Maybe Mother Goose

By Esmé Raji Codell

Illustrated by Elisa Chavarri

ALADDIN

New York   London   Toronto   Sydney   New Delhi

For the children at Stone Scholastic Academy

—E. R. C.

For my sweet Lucia

—E. C.

ALADDIN

An imprint of Simon & Schuster Children's Publishing Division

1230 Avenue of the Americas, New York, NY 10020

First Aladdin hardcover edition June 2016

Text copyright © 2016 by Esmé Raji Codell

Illustrations copyright © 2016 by Elisa Chavarri

For information about special discounts for bulk purchases, please contact Simon & Schuster Special Sales at 1-866-506-1949 or business@simonandschuster.com.

The Simon & Schuster Speakers Bureau can bring authors to your live event. For more information or to book an event contact the Simon & Schuster Speakers Bureau at 1-866-248-3049 or visit our website at www.simonspeakers.com.

Series designed by Lisa Vega

The text of this book was set in Hawaiian Aloha BTN and Carrotflower.

The illustrations for this book were digitally rendered.

Manufactured in China 0416 SCP

10 9 8 7 6 5 4 3 2 1

Library of Congress Control Number: 2015942099

ISBN 978-1-4814-4036-3 (hc)

ISBN 978-1-4814-4037-0 (eBook)

Circle time?
Yes.

Playing with friends?
Yes.

Indoor recess?

NOOOOO!

Twinkle, Twinkle

Twinkle, twinkle, little star,

How I wonder what you are!

Up above the world so high,

Like a diamond in the sky.

Twinkle, twinkle, little star,

How I wonder what you are!

Window?
Yes.

Star?
Yes.

Well, maybe.

Mary Had a Little Lamb

Mary had a little lamb,

Its fleece was white as snow,

And everywhere that Mary went,

The lamb was sure to go;

It followed her to school one day—

That was against the rule,

It made the children laugh and play

To see a lamb at school.

Mary?

Yes.

Lamb?

Yes.

Well, maybe.

Bring your pet to school day!

BONES

wee
wee
wee

Baa, Baa, Black Sheep

Baa, Baa, Black Sheep,
Have you any wool?

Yes sir, yes sir, three bags full.

One for the master,
And one for the dame,

And one for the little boy
Who lives down the lane.

Black sheep?

Yes.

Wool?

Yes.

Bags? Yes.

Camera?

NOOOOO!

Well, maybe.

Mary, Mary, Quite Contrary

Mary, Mary, quite contrary,

How does your garden grow?

With silver bells and cockleshells

And pretty maids all in a row.

Mary?

Yes.

Silver bells?

Yes.

Pretty maids?

Yes.

Wedding cake?

NOOOOO!

Well, maybe.

Sing a Song of Sixpence

Sing a song of sixpence,
A pocket full of rye;

Four-and-twenty blackbirds
Baked in a pie.

When the pie was opened,
The birds began to sing;

Wasn't that a dainty dish
To set before the king?

King?
Yes.

Pie?
Yes.

Blackbirds? Yes.

Guitar?

NOOOOO!

Well, maybe.

Four
&
Twenty

Itsy-Bitsy Spider

The itsy-bitsy spider went up
the waterspout.

Down came the rain
and washed the spider out.

Out came the sun
and dried up all the rain.

And the itsy-bitsy spider climbed up the spout again.

Waterspout?
Yes.

Spider?
Yes.

Downpour?

Yes.

Umbrella?

NOOOOO!

Well, maybe.

Listening?

Yes.

Stand and stretch?

Yes.

Playing outside?

Well, maybe.